Henry Holt and Company, LLC
Publishers since 1866
115 West 18th Street
New York, New York 10011

Text copyright © 2001 by Jeanne Willis

Illustrations copyright © 2001 by Tony Ross

First published in the United States in 2002 by Henry Holt and Company

Distributed in Canada by H. B. Fenn and Company Ltd.

Originally published in the United Kingdom in 2001 by Andersen Press Ltd.

Library of Congress Cataloging-in-Publication Data
Willis, Jeanne.
I want to be a cowgirl / Jeanne Willis and Tony Ross.
Summary: Speaking in rhyme, a little girl tells her father that she
would rather have the active outdoor life of a cowgirl than that
of a girl who stays inside quietly reading, talking, or cleaning.
[1. Cowgirls—Fiction. 2. Sex role—Fiction. 3. Stories in rhyme.]
I. Ross, Tony, ill. II. Title.
PZ8.3.W6799 Iae 2002 [E]—dc21 2001002665

ISBN 0-8050-6997-6
First American Edition—2002
Printed in Italy on acid-free paper. ∞

1 3 5 7 9 10 8 6 4 2

I WANT TO BE A COWGIRL

Jeanne Willis · Tony Ross

Henry Holt and Company

NEW YORK

I don't want to be a good girl—

Good girls have no fun.

I just want to be a cowgirl, Daddy,
What's so wrong with that?

I don't want to be a schoolgirl
With my head inside a book.

I don't want to be the kind of girl
Who likes to clean and cook.

I want to break in broncos
And twirl my rope lasso.

I want to do the kind of things
A cowgirl likes to do.

I'll drift across the prairie
And sleep beneath the moon.

I just want to be a cowgirl,
And I want to be one soon.

I'll drive my herd of cattle.
I'll hear the eagle cry.

I'll watch the wolf cubs playing
And the river running by.

The view is very different
From our twenty-story flat.

I just want to be a cowgirl, Daddy, What's so wrong with that?

The sun sets in the scrapyard—
There's a stray old dog down there.

If I screw my eyes shut tightly,
She could be my piebald mare.

I've got my shiny spurs and boots,
I've got my cowgirl hat—

I'm leaving for the Wild, Wild West.
Now what's so wrong with that?

This old town's too small for me—
I know what I must do.

I'm off to be a cowgirl, Daddy—

Come and be a cowboy too!